Rockets

MOTLEY'S CREW

Doris's Brilliant Birthday

Margaret Ryan & Margaret Chamberlain

A & C Black • London

Rockets series:

CROOK CATCHERS - Karen Wallace & Judy Brown
MOTLEY'S CREW - Margaret Ryan &
Margaret Chamberlain
MR CROC - Frank Rodgers
MRS MAGIC - Wendy Smith
MY FUNNY FAMILY - Colin West
ROVER - Chris Powling & Scoular Anderson
SILLY SAUSAGE - Michaela Morgan & Dee Shulman
WIZARD'S BOY - Scoular Anderson

First paperback edition 2001
First published 2001 in hardback by
A & C Black (Publishers) Ltd
35 Bedford Row, London WC1R 4JH

Text copyright © 2001 Margaret Ryan
Illustrations copyright © 2001 Margaret Chamberlain

The right of Margaret Ryan and Margaret Chamberlain
to be identified as author and illustrator of this
work has been asserted by them in accordance
with the Copyright, Designs and Patents Act 1988.

ISBN 0-7136-5461-9

A CIP catalogue record for this book is available
from the British Library.

Printed and bound by G. Z. Printek, Bilbao, Spain.

Chapter One

It was a very special day for Doris McNorris, the cook on board the pirate ship, *Hesmeralda*. She sang to herself as she put on her very best kilt, her very best boots, and her very best porridge perfume.

'I wonder what the crew have bought me for my birthday,' she giggled.

She skipped along to the galley to make breakfast, and was just throwing a bucketful of oats into the porridge pot when Captain Motley arrived.

Good morning, Captain. Do you know what day it is today?

The Captain looked at the date on his *Pirate Times*.

Doris gave a sigh and added a bucketful of water to the porridge pot. Surely the Captain hadn't forgotten her birthday?

She was just adding bits of old turnip for extra lumpiness when Smudger, the first mate, arrived.

Smudger looked at the date on his *Motorbike Mad* magazine. 'Tuesday,' he said.

But a special Tuesday —

You're right, Doris.

Last Tuesday in the month. It's nose-blowing Tuesday. Thanks for reminding me.

Doris gave a sigh and stirred some pongy eggs into the porridge. Surely Smudger hadn't forgotten her birthday?

She was just adding some brussel sprouts
for even more lumpiness when Kevin,
the cabin boy, arrived with Squawk on
his shoulder. Squawk rolled his eyes...

Doris ignored him and beamed at Kevin.
'Good morning, Kevin. Do you know
what day it is today?'

8

Kevin looked at the date on his *Pirate Pete* comic.

Doris gave another sigh and began to ladle out the porridge. Surely Kevin hadn't forgotten her birthday, too?

And she lit some candles and stood one in each bowl of porridge.

'No no no!' yelled Doris, and stomped back to her cabin.

Chapter Two

But the Captain and crew of the good ship *Hesmeralda* hadn't forgotten Doris's birthday. They were planning a special surprise.

Did you deliver the party invitations to the clan McNorris, Squawk?

15

Squawk flew onto the Captain's head.

'Presents?' said Captain Motley. 'Oh yes... well... of course I hadn't forgotten. I'll get her a... no, I'll get her some... or perhaps a pair of... What shall I get Doris for her birthday?'

But they weren't. They'd been so busy making their plans for Doris's birthday that they didn't see the Captain's old enemy, Captain Horatio Thunderguts, listening at an open window. And they didn't hear him laugh nastily. And they certainly didn't hear him mutter,

21

But they did hear his boots squeak as he tiptoed away.

Chapter Three

Back in her cabin, Doris had sniffed so much her hanky was soggy, so she blew her nose on the hem of her kilt. Good thing the McNorris tartan is green.

'Oh well,' she dried her eyes. 'If the crew really have forgotten my birthday, it can't be helped. I suppose I'd better go and prepare lunch.'

And she wrung out her hanky and nearly drowned a passing mouse.

Meantime, Squawk was getting worried. He went to see Doris.

Squawk thought for a moment...

Captain Motley staggered on board the *Hesmeralda*. His pink and white coat was torn and muddy.

Kevin, the cabin boy, staggered on board the *Hesmeralda*. His only T-shirt was torn and muddy.

Smudger, the first mate, staggered on board the *Hesmeralda*. He was always a mess so he didn't look much different.

'Now what are we going to do?' said the Captain. 'We spent all our money, and now we've got none left for Doris's birthday party.'

Chapter Four

The pirates sat in a circle and sighed.
Then they sat in a square and sighed
some more. They were so busy sighing
that they didn't hear the clan McNorris
come on board. They were so busy
sighing that they didn't hear them shout...

But they did hear their boots squeak
as they tiptoed towards them.
'What's that squeaky noise?' said
the Captain.
'Mice,' said the crew.

'You're wearing them,' said Kevin, but very quietly. The clan McNorris looked really fierce.

'I'm very sorry,' said the Captain. 'But there's no party.' And he told the clan McNorris what had happened.

'Absolutely no problem,' grinned Doris, and gave the whole McNorris clan a sloppy wet kiss. Squawk nearly threw up.

First the clan McNorris filled their vast tums with Doris's porridge.

'No one makes porridge like you, Doris,'
they slurped.
'That's true,' said the crew and filled
their pockets instead. Then they headed
for Thunderguts' ship, the *Saucy Stew*.

Captain Thunderguts and his crew were all in the galley laying out the party food. So they didn't hear their visitors come aboard. And they didn't see them peeping in at the window.

But they did hear their boots squeak as they tiptoed towards them.

'MICE?!' shouted the clan McNorris. 'We're not mice. We're men.' And they burst in and grabbed themselves a pirate.

Morris McNorris threw Thunderguts up into the air and forgot to catch him.

Boris McNorris threw the first mate into the sea.

Captain Motley and his crew pelted the rest of them with lumpy porridge.

Meantime Horace McNorris had got out his bagpipes and the rest of the clan McNorris began to dance. Up and down the deck they danced. Up and down. Up and down.

Captain Horatio Thunderguts didn't think so.

'Just look at the mess of my ship,' he yelled from underneath three of the clan McNorris. 'The Chief Pirate will boil me in oil when he sees this.'

'Serves you right for trying to mess up my birthday party,' grinned Doris. 'But I forgive you. Would you like some food?' 'Oh, go on then,' said Captain Thunderguts.

Doris stuffed his mouth with lumpy porridge.

I knew you'd like it. Have some more. I want everyone to enjoy my brilliant birthday!